THE BIG GUST

by Andrew Clements
illustrated by Terry Widener

HOUGHTON MIFFLIN

BOSTON

It was just another day in Mayville. Folks were doing the things that they did in the summer. And then that one big gust came through.

Everyone in Mayville knows where they were at the time.

Jean Adams had a dog named Clipper. Jean often said, "That name is perfect for my dog. I always have to clip her hair and nails."

When the big gust came, in fact, Clipper was getting clipped. She was also yawning. The wind blew into her mouth.

Clipper blew up until she was ten times bigger than before. Then away she went. Jean went after her.

It wasn't long before the police got a call. "Help! I'm being chased by a barking balloon with hair ribbons!" yelled the caller.

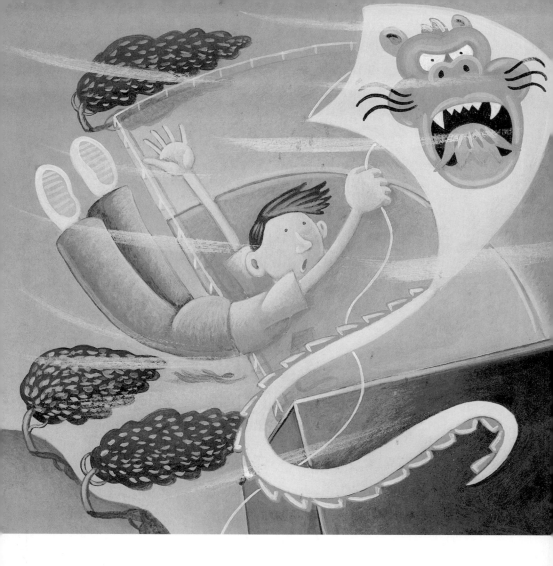

Tommy James was flying his new kite at the ball
field. When the big gust came, Tommy held on
tight. He went on a wild kite ride to the schoolyard.

Tommy saw the flagpole. He looped his legs and then the string around it. Then he slid down to the ground. He was safe and sound, but he had to leave the kite behind.

Elsie Chen was watering her garden. When the big gust came, it swept the hat off her head. Elsie turned around to see where her hat went.

When she turned back, her garden was on the roof of the house next door.

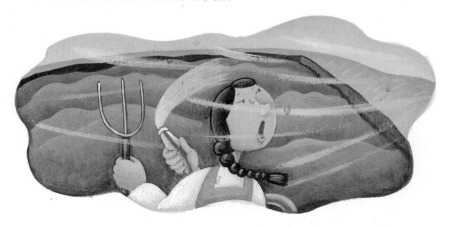

"Oh, good," thought Elsie. "Now my tomatoes are closer to the sun. I'll just get a longer hose and a tall ladder from the hardware store. I wonder if my neighbors will mind."

They didn't. Elsie's tomatoes got a lot of sunshine, water, and special attention up on that roof. Then they won first prize at the county fair!

At the school gym, some kids were playing kickball. When the big gust came, the doors flew open. You'll never guess what blew in. It was a pond, with three ducks, six lily pads, three frogs, and one tall man in a little red rowboat!

The tall man stayed to play water polo with the
kids. The ducks and frogs watched the game from the
red rowboat. The lily pads just sat there, taking up
space.

Bob Belcher was mowing his lawn. When the big
gust came, Bob and his mower took off like a driver
and a racing car.

Together they cut a path through six front yards
and a blackberry thicket.

12

The big gust blew all the grass Bob mowed to the town library. It formed a pile on the front steps.

Soon a bunch of kids were reading their books on that soft, delicious-smelling green carpet.

Over at the Sport Shop, Jane Asher was putting some tennis balls on the shelf. When the big gust came, they blew off the shelf and then blew all the way to Chestertown, along with other balls of all shapes and sizes.

That afternoon there was a news flash from
Chestertown. "Tim Lewis here in the middle of a
hailstorm. Some hailstones are as big as tennis
balls. I mean softballs. No, wait a minute . . .
footballs! Could they be as big as bowling balls?
Oh no, BASKETBALLS! HELP!"

Gary Jones was all set to fix his picket fence.

When the big gust came, every single picket and a whole box of nails went up in a jumble. But when they came down, Gary had a new fence. And he'd never even picked up his hammer!

After that, Gary tried to build fences by juggling pickets, nails, and his hammer. As you might guess, he became a better juggler than a fence builder. So he joined the circus when it came to town.

As fast as it came, the big gust left town. But the folks in Mayville will never forget that windy day.

Strange things have happened since then. But nothing has been as wild as that one big gust!

18